CAPTURED

A Story of Love and Overcoming

A Film Script by

Carlos "KRL" Mera

LEGAL PAGE

Captured
A story of Love and Overcoming.
A Film Script by:
Carlos "KRL" Mera

AUTHOR'S BIOGRAPHY

Carlos Mera, also known as KRL, is a writer, actor, producer/Dj of electronic music, and owner of his own record label "KRL Records".

Carlos Mera was born in Cartagena, Colombia, and raised in Barranquilla, Colombia. His identity as KRL was created in 2007. Since 2009 KRL has released music in the form of albums and singles.

In 2016 KRL released the album #Tangible! from which 5 singles came out and all reached #1 in Napster Latino making this album a success.

Until 2020 KRL has released more than 28 singles with various collaborations, being "Fight for What Is Right (Radio Edit)" one of their best songs, having "Emarie" (professional singer who worked with Avicii on "Malo") as vocal singer, and being mastered in Germany by "Klaas" one of the producers of "Infinity 2008"

In 2022 "Fight for What Is Right (Radio Edit)" won Best EDM Song of 2022 at the Psychedelic Music and Film Festival in New York City.

THANKS

The story of **Captured** begins with my desire to tell an action story with several ingredients, showing the despair and trauma that the protagonists of this story go through. It was written thinking of making this an independent film, using film language and taking into account the actors who will play the characters in this story.

For this reason, my thanks go to all the people who helped to develop this project as such, to my fellow actors who contributed with many brainstorming ideas as they wanted their characters and their outcome to be.

I dedicate this book to my mother **Maria Cristina Serpa Sfeir**, who from heaven sees all my triumphs and I know that you are happy for all the achievements that I have achieved, mommy.

This book is also dedicated to my father **Mario Orlando Mera Fernandez**, who was the first writer I met, and who inspired me to write since I was a child, thank you dad.

Many times I found myself immersed in the world of **Captured**, imagining what words this character would use, how he would react and above all how to make each scene special, how to give the story a cliffhanger and make it interesting.

Now I leave it up to you so that you can also enter the world of **Captured** and let yourself be **Captured** by this story, enjoy it!

Table of Contents

CAPTURED 3

LEGAL PAGE 4

AUTHOR'S BIOGRAPHY 5

THANKS 7

Table of Contents 8

Scene 1: Exterior - Forest - Day 11

Scene 2: Interior Basement - Night 13

Scene 3: New York City - Interior Room - Day 17

Scene 4 - Interior - Hospital Room - Day 20

Scene 5 - Interior - Amelia's House - Day 25

Scene 6 - Exterior - New York City - Afternoon 28

Scene 7 - Interior - House "The Boss" - Afternoon 32

Scene 8 - Interior - Hospital Room - Night 34

Scene 9 - Interior Police Office - Day 41

Scene 10 - Exterior - Central Park - New York City 44

Scene 11 - Interior - Hotel Room - Day 52

Scene 12 - Interior - Angelica's Office - Day	56
Scene 13 - Interior Police Office - Day	60
Scene 14 - Exterior New York City - Day	63
Scene 15 - Interior - Basement - Day	67
Scene 16 - Interior Basement - Night	75
Scene 17 - Interior - The Boss House - Day	76
Scene 18 - Interior - Basement - Day	81
Scene 19 - Interior - House The Boss - Day	86
Scene 20 - Interior - House The Boss - Day	91
Scene 21 - Interior - Basement - Day	95
Scene 22 - Interior - House The Boss - Day	98
Scene 23 - Interior - House The Boss - Day	104
Scene 24 - Interior - House The Boss - Day	108
Scene 25 - Various Locations -	115
Scene 26 - Post Credits 1 - Exterior - Beach/Pool	116
Scene 27 - Post Credits 2 - Interior - Jail Women -	118

Scene 1: Exterior - Forest - Day

Walter (police) is undercover (without police clothes and without a gun) looking for the place where "El Jefe" lives and his criminal organization and is surprised by Franco (El Hacker) , one of the criminals. Walter starts running.
Walter runs through the woods while he is being chased by Franco.

Walter stumbles and falls, at this moment Franco arrives and takes advantage and kicks him, hitting him in the stomach. Walter is thrown by the kick and falls to the ground. Walter starts to drag.

FRANCO

What? Did you think you were going to run away?
What are you doing here? What are you looking for?

Walter gets up and throws a fist at Franco, he falls to the floor. Walter jumps on him and begins to punch him quite a bit, until Franco is unconscious.

At that precise moment Trap appears, he is not armed either, but he starts running where Walter is. Trap catches up to Walter and grabs him from behind.

TRAP

You idiot, stop running!

Walter throws a fist at Trap but he dodges it, and returns another, hitting him in the stomach.

TRAP

Who the hell are you? And what are you doing here?

Walter takes advantage and hits him in the face, Trap turns his body into a 180 degree turn.
At that moment Christopher arrives with a gun and shoots into the air.

CHRISTOPHER

Enough! The next shot won't be into the air, so put your hands up and give yourself up.

Walter raises his hands.

Scene 2: Interior Basement - Night

Walter is found tied up and head down. There is a light over his head, when he lifts it up you can see his injured face, his nose is bleeding, his left eye is black, blood is coming out of his mouth. Walter has been tortured.

TRAP

We already know that you are a fucking policeman, and that you participated in the investigation of the bank robbery.

FRANCO

And thanks to my hacking into your account, we know that Ramón helped them in that investigation.

CHRISTOPHER

What the hell are you looking for here? huh? Do you think a single policeman can stop us? fool!

WALTER

How many times do I have to tell you, I don't know anything! I don't know what you're talking about!

At that moment El Jefe arrives, his back is seen up to the height of his shoulders, his face is not shown. Behind him comes his wife, "La Jefa" , a shot of their faces is seen.

EL JEFE

Well, well, What we are going to do official Walter is very simple. You have two options: tell us everything right now, or tell us everything, when your whole family is here kidnapped and tortured! it 's up to you!

LA JEFA

Look Walter, if I were you, I'd leave my family out of this and I would tell everything that I know.

EL JEFE

Who the fuck! told you that you could say anything here?

LA JEFA

Do not shout at me! okay? and not in front of them! I remind you that everything you have has been thanks to me! you owe it to me! You respect me! Mother Fucker!

EL JEFE

Excuse me, I just don't want you involved in this! the less you know the better!

LA JEFA

You know that I know everything! everything! that happens in this house! You can't hide anything from me!

There is silence...

At that moment the security camera is seen, and we see that on the other side of the camera there is a mysterious character watching everything that happens, you can't see his face because he has his back turned.

Walter realizes that he is in a very difficult situation, but he knows that he does not want to put his family in danger.

WALTER

Alright! I'll tell you everything! but promise me you'll leave my family out of this!

Walter pauses.

WALTER

It all started when I received a call from Ramón Cortez, he asked me to meet and that he wanted to collaborate with the police, he told me that he suspected his wife, Lorena and he thought that she was participating in a bank robbery, he told me that he had a plan to get out of all this. It was then that...

We jump to a Flashback (memory) in the next scene.

Scene 3: New York City - Interior Room - Day

Walter's Voice Over:

(12 hours had passed since Ramón had pretended to be dead) Walter enters a room, where Ramón is lying face down. Walter looks everywhere making sure there is no one. Walter touches Ramón's body twice.

WALTER

Who would have thought that your plan would turn out so well.

At that moment Ramón gets up.

WALTER

At this moment everyone believes that Ramón Cortez is dead.

RAMÓN

Walter, you know why I'm doing this. You know who the real criminals are, with your help we are going to bring them to justice.

WALTER

Here are the clothes and your new ID. You also have the key and the address of the hotel where you are going to hide. You are going to stay there until I or Mariana give you new instructions. I just hope all of this has been worth it.

(Ramón is changing his clothes, while he listens to Walter's instructions. In the package that Walter gives him is the new clothes, some documents and some cash.)

RAMÓN

Trust me, we are doing the right thing.

WALTER

There you also have your part of the money from the robbery, 5 million dollars, do you understand that this money must be returned to the police?

RAMÓN

Walter, my plan is to get out of all this clean. For now we need this money to execute our plans.

WALTER

Okay whatever! When leaving here you must not use a cell phone or credit cards, you must pay everything in cash.

(There is silence...)

RAMÓN

How, how is Lorraine?

WALTER

Lorena is in an induced coma, her injuries are not fatal, but for your sake and hers, it is better that she recovers.

RAMÓN

I never wanted to hurt her, it's my disease! you know! I had a hallucination, it wasn't her who I wanted to hurt!

WALTER

Remember that for no reason should you communicate with her, with her or with anyone.

At that moment the scene changes and Lorena can be seen in the hospital bed recovering from her injuries.

Scene 4 - Interior - Hospital Room - Day
Walter's Voice Over:
(A week after Ramón had injured Lorena, Police Director Edgardo Martinez was at her side when she woke up from a coma)

She is lying on the table wearing a white hospital gown, she has one or two small band-aids on her face, and a very large bandage all over her chest that cannot be seen well.

Walter's Voice Over:
(Edgardo, the Chief of Police, had visited the hospital every day to see Lorena's condition. That day she was lucky to be there at the right time)

Edgardo had a small notebook in his hand and was writing something. Lorena wakes up for the first time after what happened.

LORRAINE

ahh.. where am I? What happened to me?

EDGARDO

Mrs. Lorena, I am Director Edgardo Martinez, you were found with knife wounds, fortunately you are already recovering.

Lorena changes the expression on her face to anger and hatred.

LORRAINE

Ramón did this to me, right? Where is that son of a bitch?

EDGARDO

Lady calm down.

There was a pause to which Lorena managed to calm her nerves.

EDGARDO

I'm sorry to tell you that your husband,
Ramón Cortez, is dead.

Lorena changes her expression from anger to pain.

LORRAINE

What? What happened?

EDGARDO

After fleeing, he was found in a residence, where some girls thought that he was going to attack them, like you, but his body could not resist anymore and he died at that moment.

LORRAINE

He, he needed psychiatric help, I tried to help him,
but his sickness took hold of him.

EDGARDO

That's right Mrs. Lorena, let me tell you, that
We understand that you were a victim of what happened.

Lorena shakes her head, agreeing with the director
from the police.

EDGARDO

I also inform you that we found a part
of the money from the bank robbery in your possession.

LORRAINE

Detective, that money is going to help me to be able to
redo my life, start from scratch again.

EDGARDO

Let me finish talking...
(Pause)

Lorena looks seriously at the detective, while she is there, he takes out some handcuffs and uses them to tie Lorena to the hospital bed.

EDGARDO

You are under arrest for the bank robbery. You will remain in this hospital until you recover and can face justice. In the meantime, you are entitled to a lawyer and keep quiet. Anything you say can be used against you.

When he finished saying this, the detective stands up and he walks to the door.

LORRAINE

What? You are crazy! you can't do that to me! You already have the money! Set me free!

The detective returns to Lorena and answers her. Even if you voluntarily give up the money, that doesn't mean you haven't committed a crime. You have to face the justice of this country.

Scene 5 - Interior - Amelia's House - Day

Amelia (Ramon's sister) is at her house with her husband preparing to go out and visit Lorena at the hospital.

AMELIA

Emmanuel...are you ready yet? We are going to visit Lorena at the hospital today! remember!

EMANUEL

Yeah! Yes my love! I know! but I'm afraid to see how her reaction will be! Anyway, I'm going to shower and get ready, wait for me!

AMELIA

Well hurry up! She has restricted visits today.

Amelia stays in the living room, when she hears a voice.

EMILIA (2 PERSONALITY)

Amelia....Amelia....Amelia.......

AMELIA

What? Who calls me? Who's there?

Amelia approaches the mirror and manages to see another person speaking to her.

EMILIA (2 PERSONALITY)

Amelia...it's me, Emilia...I came to remind you that Lorena, is the one to blame for the death of your brother Ramón.

AMELIA

What? Emila? but... if Lorena was a victim, My brother had a hallucination! she didn't kill him!

EMILIA (2 PERSONALITY)

Oh...Amelia, you know that Lorena involved him in a bank robbery, she was the one who made him an accomplice in that robbery. She is to blame for his death!

AMELIA

No.. no.. That 's not true! Ramón almost killed her! She is alive by a miracle! Why do you say those things to me?

EMILIA (2 PERSONALITY)

Today! that you're going to see her again, it's your chance to avenge Ramón's death, if you don't do it, I'll do it!

AMELIA

What? No! get out! I do not know who you are! but get out of here! now!

EMANUEL

I am ready! Amelia! I'm ready now!
Who were you talking to?

AMELIA

Ah ok! It was the neighbor! Yes, she called me to gossip! you know how she is! I send her to hell! I'm not for those things right now! let's go then!

Scene 6 - Exterior - New York City - Afternoon

Walter's Voice Over:

(24 hours had passed since Ramón's last hallucination, he walked through the streets of New York, he arrived at a park and sat down, he began to analyze his situation, he felt alone, he remembered his daughter, he imagined the pain she must be feeling, but he knew that for her safety it was best not to communicate with her)

Ramón looks at the hotel card "Steward Hotel" he says, he gets up and leaves the park, he starts looking for a place to take the Subway that will take him to the hotel.

Ramón arrives at the hotel, enters the elevator, looks at the room number, and selects the floor he goes to.

When Ramón opens the bedroom door, he realizes
that apparently someone is already there, he hears the sound of the television on, as well as the lights on.

When Ramón enters he is surprised by Mariana, who is getting dressed and in a brassier. Mariana did not listen when Ramón entered the room because she was listening to music with headphones.

RAMÓN

Ooh wow! What a pity! I'm sorry!

When Mariana notices him, she takes off her headphones, puts on a T-shirt and says:

MARIANA

Ramon Cortez! Do not worry, take it easy!
I was changing into civilian clothes.

RAMÓN

I'm ashamed, Mrs. Mariana,
I didn't think you would be here.

MARIANA

Ramón, you can only call me Mariana,
Take away the ma'am please!

RAMÓN

Alright! Mariana, at least I'm glad to see and talk to someone! All this has been very traumatic.

MARIANA

Ramón... of course! that's why I'm here
Come sit down, do you want a drink?

RAMÓN

Do you have water?

MARIANA

Of course! I will bring it to you!

Mariana gets up and leaves the frame, goes to look for the water for Ramón meanwhile she keeps talking to him.

MARIANA

Walter told me that you had already left and were heading here. My job today is to give you the instructions that you must follow to the letter. After that I can go and leave you alone. Take! here is the water

Instead of grabbing the water, Ramón grabs Mariana's hand. He stands up and very close to Mariana's face.

RAMÓN

I really don't want you to leave me alone
This bed is too big for me!

Mariana stays still, her face shows that she is not indifferent to Ramón. Ramón continues to hold her left hand and with her right he caresses her hair.

MARIANA

I guess you must be hungry
and not exactly food!

Mariana takes the initiative and gives Ramón a kiss. After the kiss they walk away and look into each other's eyes. Ramón now takes the initiative and gives Mariana a more passionate kiss.

They both take off their remaining clothes.

Scene 7 - Interior - "El Jefe" House - Afternoon

El Jefe is at his house and receives a mysterious call.

EL JEFE

Hello, tell me, Eagle, I'm listening..

EAGLE

How is the operation going to recover the 5 million from the bank?

EL JEFE

We have a plan! We already know that Ramón faked his death, we are going to kidnap his family so that he comes out of his hiding place and gives us that money.

EAGLE

That's good!, but 5 million is little compared to what we can have with that database, as the decryption goes.

EL JEFE

We have our expert hacker on that! You have to understand that it's not as easy and fast as you think, it takes time, I'll keep you posted!

EAGLE

I just hope you don't leave any loose ends out there...

I don't want mistakes this time...

Scene 8 - Interior - Hospital Room - Night

(Two weeks after Lorena was admitted to the hospital)

Lorena is recovering in the hospital, she is sedated, her sister Carolina is sitting next to her, accompanying her. Amelia and Emanuel arrive to visit her.

AMELIA

Good morning! I'm Amelia Cortez, this is my husband Emanuel Cortez, we came to visit Raquel.

Carolina stands up.

CAROLINA

Oh! The Cortez family comes to see the damage that Ramón did, right?

EMANUEL

Sweetheart, you must be Carolina, Lorena's sister... believe me we are very sorry for this situation, that's why we are here, we want to apologize for Ramón's actions, since he cannot.

CAROLINA

Ramón's actions? Mister? I remind you, he almost killed my sister! It's a miracle that she's fighting for her life right now!

AMELIA

Girl, we know, and we are very hurt by this situation, but understand my brother, he had mental problems, he loved Lorena very much, he was hopelessly in love with her.

CAROLINA

So in love he was,that he stabbed her multiple times...

AMELIA

Sweetheart, understand, my brother was exposed to a hyper stressful and traumatic situation, which led him to develop a severe hallucination episode! He could not distinguish between what was real and what was not.

EMANUEL

That's how it is! Ramón struggled for many years with his mental health and managed to get ahead, but he had a relapse at that time.

AMELIA

That's why we're here! because we are worried about Lorena, we want everything to be cleared up!

CAROLINA

Well look! I understand absolutely nothing of what you are telling me! The only thing I know! is that my sister is in recovery! She is now sedated! she can't talk to you! and that's why I ask you to go! and leave us alone!

AMELIA

Alright! we are leaving, but believe me we are very worried! and we will be pending any news!

Amelia and Emanuel leave the room. It gets dark and Carolina continues to accompany her sister, she is using her cell phone, when Lorena wakes up... Lorena makes sounds that tell Carolina that she is waking up.

CAROLINA

Sister, calm down! I am here with you. You have to be strong and recover from all this... it's all Ramón's fault... he did this to you! He ratted you out to the police! I don't understand how you fell in love with that idiot!

LORRAINE

Caro! Thank you for accompanying me, little sister, Ramón... he was my husband, he and I had happy moments, he is no longer here! Leave him alone! respect his memory and his death!

CAROLINA

Respect him? And why doesn't he respect you? huh?

LORRAINE

Carolina, Ramón suffered from mental illness. The last thing we lived together was very stressful for him, and that made his situation worse. He had a relapse, I assure you he didn't want to hurt me, he was having a hallucination when things happened.

CAROLINA

Hallucination? What's that?

LORRAINE

A hallucination occurs when the mind perceives things whose existence is not real, but to the person they are very true.

CAROLINA

I don't understand anything there! Today the Cortez family came to visit you, and they explained the same thing to me, but that for me is to be crazy! you married a madman! and there you have the consequences.

LORRAINE

Carolina! It's too late! and I need to rest! good night!

Carolina takes out her cell phone and begins to have fun with it. At that moment Franco appears disguised as a nurse.

FRANCO

Good evening, sorry for the time. We received an order and we must move Mrs. Lorena to another room with greater protection.

Carolina, put her cell phone away and get up.

CAROLINA

What? You are crazy! my sister,
You're not going to take her anywhere!

FRANCO

Miss, what a shame with you, I'm just doing my job and following the orders they gave me!

CAROLINA

Well I don't give a damn!
Can't you see that my sister is weak and recovering?

FRANCO

We know, miss, but it was a police order, we must move her to a more secure area.

At that moment, Trap enters the room, he stands next to Carolina.

TRAP

Excuse me, I need you to sign an authorization,
to my partner.

CAROLINA

Well! I'm not going to sign anything.

FRANCO

Miss, please help me with your signature here!

Franco takes out a handkerchief and puts it in Carolina's mouth, causing her to lose consciousness.

LORRAINE

What? What are you doing to my sister? Who are you?

Franco takes out an injection and puts it into the tube that Lorena has on.

FRANCO

Mrs. Lorena, you will go with us for a while,
¡El Jefe needs your services again!

Lorena is unconscious and falls asleep.

CHRISTOPHER

Gentlemen, there is no one outside. Put Lorena in a wheelchair, I'll get her sister out the back.

Scene 9 - Interior Police Office - Day

Police Chief Edgardo Martinez arrives at the office and meets Javier and Officer Juana Zarante.

EDGARDO

Good morning my people, how did you wake up today? Will we have good news? Tell me yes, please!

ZARANTE

Good morning boss.

EDGARDO

Zarante, I need you to contact Officer Walter immediately and ask him how he is doing with his investigation.

ZARANTE

Mr. Martinez, I have been trying to contact Officer Walter since last night and I haven't been able to make it.

EDGARD

Since last night? Well, call his house, his family to see what they say.

ZARANTE

I already did it boss, but Officer Walter hasn't been home for two days. And he has not communicated with them either.

EDGARDO

Two days? What are you trying to tell me?
Is Walter missing? or what?

ZARANTE

Well boss, we are waiting the necessary time
to declare him missing.

EDGARDO

And how is it that until now I found out about this? huh?
Javier, tell me where is officer Mariana?
I need to speak to her urgently.

JAVIER

Mr. Martinez, Officer Mariana has not been answering the phone. She's been on an undercover operation since last night.

EDGARD

What is Javier talking about?
What operation is that? huh?

JAVIER

I don't know very well, it's better that when she arrives, she explains herself.

Edgardo raises his voice and says:

EDGARD

How is it possible that she is in an operation of which I have no idea? huh? What is going on in this office?
(there is a silence)

EDGARDO

Answer Javier! don't be silent!

JAVIER

What can I tell you boss,
I'll keep trying to get in touch with her.
As soon as I have more information, I will inform you.

EDGARDO

Zarante, I need you to keep me posted
of what happens with Walter, I need to be aware
everything that happens in this office.

ZARANTE

Of course, boss! I'm going to investigate
What is going on with Walter..

Scene 10 - Exterior - Central Park -
New York City - Early in the morning.

Amelia (Ramon's sister) is exercising and walking in Central Park early in the morning together with her husband Emanuel.

AMELIA

oh wow, wait, let's stop here for a moment.

EMANUEL

It's ok, let me know when you're ready,
I want to take you to a special place!

AMELIA

what? special place? let 's see?
What site is that?

EMANUEL

It is a place that you will love and it is very special!

AMELIA

No, I'm already all intrigued,
take me to that special place! already!

Emanuel takes Amelia to the Bow Bridge in Central Park.

EMANUEL

I am bringing you to the jewel in the Crown of Central Park, this is the Bow Bridge.

AMELIA

Yes wow how beautiful!

EMANUEL

It was built in 1862, it is the second oldest cast iron bridge in America.

AMELIA

Wow, but how do you have so much information!
oh .. I think this place is beautiful!

EMANUEL

Since I know you like movies, you have to know that here a scene for Spiderman 3 was filmed with Tobey Maguire and Kristen Dunst. In the scene Mary Jane breaks up and ends up with Peter Parker.

AMELIA

Don't even think of doing something like that to me, ever!
You know I couldn't live without you! much less now.

EMANUEL

Of course not my beloved Amelia, in fact I want to tell you
that I will be by your side until the day I die
and you will always be able to count on me.

Emanuel takes some flowers out of his backpack and hands them to Amelia.

AMELIA

Ah, Emanuel of my heart those
beautiful flowers, thank you very much!

Amelia pauses, her eyes watering.

AMELIA

You know? I miss my brother, Ramón, a lot. I transmitted
my love for cinema and the arts to him. and he liked all that
world! It makes me very sad to know that his dreams did not
come true, that he did not have the time or the opportunity
to try, even if it was to appear as an extra in a movie!
Why is life like this?

EMANUEL

Amelia you have to understand that you can't live your brother's life! it is necessary to let each one search and decide what he wants to do with his life.

AMELIA

I know I know! but I still miss him and wanted to see him happy, healthy and next to a good woman! Not like that Lorraine! that all she did was cause him to die! Nooo what pain I have! I'm not over it yet!

Amelia hugs Emanuel and starts to cry. She sees a man from behind, who is watching them, his face is not shown and it is not known who he is. While that is happening, Franco, Trampa and Christopher arrive in a van to Central Park.

FRANCO

Well gentlemen! According to the GPS on his cell phone, Ramón's sister is 500 feet from where we are.

CHRISTOPHER

We need to be very careful that no one sees our faces, Did you bring the masks?

TRAP

Of course! What do you think? They're over here!
I'm not going to expose myself in broad daylight!
I also brought the wheelchairs.

CHRISTOPHER

Ready, then, let's Capture them!

The 3 get out of the car and start walking. Arrive at Bow Bridge.

FRANCO

Gentlemen, there is Amelia, Ramón's sister.

CHRISTOPHER

That must be her husband.

TRAP

Well, we did come for that one too,
that one is coming with us today!

CHRISTOPHER

Trap, you go to the other side of the bridge and I'll get closer
on this side here and I talk to the lady.

TRAP

Ready! Franco be aware, so that you can approach with the wheelchairs ready to take them to the van.

CHRISTOPHER

One moment! Who has the chloroform? Or how do you think we are going to make them faint?

TRAP

Don't worry about that! I have here handkerchiefs impregnated with chloroform.

FRANCO

We already have everything ready! Now, you have to do things quickly without making a fuss.

Christopher approaches Amelia and says:

CHRISTOPHER

What a pity to interrupt you, but I see that the lady is crying, and she moves me very much. Let me give her this handkerchief to dry her tears.

At that moment, Amelia walks away from Emanuel to talk to the man.

AMELIA

Thank you very much sir, but I'm fine now.

CHRISTOPHER

Excuse me for insisting ma'am, but you remind me a lot of my sister, and I have never, ever liked to see her cry, have it and dry those tears.

Amelia takes the handkerchief and holds it close to her face.

AMELIA

Oh sir, this handkerchief smells so bad!

At that moment Amelia loses consciousness and falls unconscious and is grabbed by Christopher. At the same moment Trampa approaches from behind with the anonymous mask on and with another handkerchief and puts it on Emanuel from behind.

TRAP

Now yes! Old asshole, you're going with us too!

Trap brought a wheelchair with him and made Emanuel sit on the chair. Then Franco approaches (who also is wearing an Anonymous mask) with another chair and sits Amelia on it and they are taken to the van.

While they are doing that, a mysterious person is seen from behind, witnessing everything that happened.

Scene 11 - Interior - Hotel Room - Day

The shot begins with Mariana on top of Ramón. Ramón is hallucinating with Raquel. Ramón makes noises while he sleeps.

MARIANA

Ramón! Ramón, are you okay? You had a nightmare! you were calling Lorraine!

RAMÓN

huh? Sorry, I didn't sleep well. I need to talk to my psychiatrist, I need to continue with my treatment. I don't want to have another relapse, and hurt you.

MARIANA

It's ok but be very careful, the police are still looking for you. The previous detective was removed from the case and now it is the same director, Edgardo Martinez, who is in charge.

At that moment Mariana receives a call, she gets out of bed, it is her co-worker, Javier.

MARIANA

Javier, tell me, what's going on?

JAVIER

Mariana, where are you? they need you right now!

MARIANA

Come on but what happened? I'm going there!

JAVIER

Apparently they have captured Lorena,
her sister and Ramón relatives.

MARIANA

What? and Walter where is he?
I have not been able to communicate with him!

JAVIER

Detective Walter is missing, we don't know his whereabouts.
We thought something had happened to you, too!

MARIANA

Relax, I'm fine! I'm going there!

Mariana looks at Ramón, who is on the floor with the head down!

MARIANA

Ramón! take it easy! you have to be strong, we have to stick with the plan! Look, I'm going to give you this cell phone, so I can communicate with you, don't do anything without consulting me first, okay?

Ramón shakes his head and they kiss goodbye.

Two hours later, Ramón uses his cell phone to access Facebook and send a message to his psychiatrist.
You can see the message that says:

(Dr. Angelica, I'm Ramón Cortez, I need to talk to you, can I come to your office today?)

Angelica replies:
(Ramón Cortez? Is it really you?)
Ramón answers:
(Yes it's me! Doctor Angelica, can I call you now?)
Angelica replies:
(Of course, call me now!)

RAMÓN

Doctor how are you?

ANGELICA

Ramon! How are you?

RAMÓN

Doctor, can I go to your office today?

ANGELICA

Today? Let me see! My last appointment is at 3 in the afternoon, can you come at 4? You will be my last patient.

RAMÓN

Of course! I'll be there at 4! Please don't tell anyone I'm going to be there! I'll explain everything later!

Scene 12 - Interior - Angelica's Office - Day

Ramón is lying on a sofa, and Dr. Angelica next to him in one of his psychiatric sessions.

RAMÓN

Angelica, doctor, I don't know what to call you anymore, thank you for receiving me and listening to me.

ANGELICA

Ramón, regardless of what happens between us, you know that I have always been aware of your evolution and your recovery.

RAMÓN

Before I tell you everything, I want to know about my daughter, Valeria. How is she?

ANGELICA

At this point you come to remember your daughter, Ramón. Valeria left the country two weeks ago, she couldn't take the pressure, she needed to rest and get away from everything!

RAMÓN

What? Where did she go? When I tell you everything, you'll understand why I did what I did, and how things happened.

ANGELICA

Okay, tell me, have you hallucinated again?

RAMÓN

Yeah! I was captured, my mom, my dad, Lorena, all of them, (silence) Doctor, I didn't kill her! Why would I hurt her? She is my wife now, I love her.

ANGELICA

She is a snake that deceived and manipulated you, Ramón.

RAMÓN

I understand that you don't like her, in a way, she got in the way of our relationship. What I don't understand is why I had that hallucination? Everything seemed so real.

ANGELICA

Sometimes a hallucination is our brain's way of forcing us to face the things we are running from in our reality. (silence) Tell me, have you run from something lately?

RAMÓN

The police and the fucking hackers are chasing me, what do you think? My hallucination came true!

ANGELICA

I'm so sorry, Ramon.
How long ago did the hallucination happen?

RAMÓN

It's been more than two weeks now. I had to fake my death, they helped me, but... I can't tell you who.

ANGELICA

Why are you here talking to me then?

RAMÓN

I haven't been able to sleep well, I've been like this for 4 nights, I'm afraid of hallucinating again, of hurting more people, I need those fucking pills!

ANGELICA

Ramón, remember that despite your illness, if you follow the treatment as it should be, you can live a normal life, and make the decisions that you consider best for yourself, just like everyone else does.

RAMÓN

That is what I want the most, doctor, to have a normal life, next to my family and live happily and in peace.

ANGELICA

We were your family, but, Ok, I understand, Here are the pills, keep in mind that this treatment cannot be interrupted! You should take two before bed. Wait a minute, I'll be right back.

(Angelica walks away and takes out a cell phone, she writes a message of text that says:
"Ramón is with me, how soon will you arrive?)

She then pours a cup of green tea, adds a substance to the tea and brings it to Ramón. She puts the tea on a tray and next to her her cell phone. She then puts the tray on the table near Ramón.

ANGELICA

I prepared this special tea for you to relax.

(At that moment a message arrives on her cell phone)
"in 5 minutes we are there"
(Ramón manages to read the message)

RAMÓN

Doctor? Who's coming here?
Did you tell someone that I am here?

ANGELICA

I'm sorry Ramón, they have threatened me, and under their surveillance, I didn't know what to do, I'm scared, they are very dangerous!

RAMÓN

Of course they are dangerous! You have no idea of the damage you are doing to me, you know what?
You got this yourself...

(At that moment Ramón grabs a vase and hits Dr. Angelica on the head, she falls and loses consciousness)
(At that moment Ramón takes the opportunity to run out of the place)

Scene 13 - Interior Police Office - Day

Officer Sara Vega rushes to the police office. Director Martinez and officers Zarante and Javier are there.

SARA

Mr. Martinez, have you heard?

EDGARDO

Heard what Vega?

SARA

Mariana, Mr. Martinez, she had an attack,
that's why she didn't answer the calls.

EDGARDO

What are you talking about, Vega?

SARA

It's all over the news,
Times Square is paralyzed.
Turn on the TV and see it for yourself.

ZARANTE

I'll take care of it, I'll put it right away.

On the television a presenter is seen giving the news of Mariana's death.

NEWS PRESENTER

She... she was found seriously injured in the Times Square area. It is presumed that the attack was carried out by a middle-aged white-skinned man, with an illegal weapon, from the suburbs of the city. Officer Romero was taken by paramedics to the nearest hospital, where she was declared dead, minutes after her arrival. The suspect escaped and the police are gathering information to find her whereabouts.
Very unfortunate news.
On the other hand, President Biden announced new measures in the face of the immigration crisis that the country is experiencing...

Zarante turns off the television.

ZARANTE

How could all this have happened?
and we found out on the news? huh?

SARA

Commander, you know that, that is not our jurisdiction,
we can’t get involved with that department.

EDGARDO

But the victim was our partner,
we should have been there. Even more so, if we already had some information. Javier, you mentioned that Mariana was undergoing an undercover operation.
What the hell is going on? Tell us!

JAVIER

Mr. Martinez, the truth is I didn't want to get involved in this. But I accidentally overheard a conversation between Mariana and Walter. They helped Ramón Cortez to fake his death. He is alive, Mr. Martinez.

EDGARD

Don't be stupid Javier, how is he going to be alive if he was pronounced dead, and his body was taken away.

JAVIER

Boss, from what I could understand, they gave him a drug that slows down his heartbeat, so he could pass for dead, then they were going to inject him with adrenaline and wake him up.

EDGARDO

Wait there! Javier! You are telling me that we were deceived, and they saw our faces as idiots!
Did either of you two know about that?

SARA

No, Mr. Martinez, I did not know and I did not hear anything! I swear! You know how serious I am about those things.

ZARANTE

Me neither, boss, it's the first time I've heard something like that. If I had known I would have told you.
You know how I work.

JAVIER

Ramón Cortez never died boss, it was all a plan so he could escape from the hackers who had kidnapped him and his wife Lorena. It seems something went wrong between the two of them. Ramón suffers from a mental illness or something like that, I heard them say.

EDGARDO

Do you know the seriousness of what you are telling me?
Javier? What happened to Walter, where is he?

JAVIER

Mr. Martinez, last thing I heard, Walter was looking for the house of the head of the criminal hacker organization. It is most likely that he was Captured by them.

EDGARDO

If something happens to Detective Walter, you will be responsible for that. Where is Ramón Cortez right now and why if he is alive he is not in police custody?

JAVIER

Ramón was in Mariana's custody. When I spoke to her, she told me that she was heading towards this office. Unfortunately she never came.

EDGARDO

Stop there, you told me that you hadn't talked to her, so you lied to me?

EDGARDO

Why do you think of doing something like that?
How the hell you decide to work alone,
on your own, like this isn't a team!
We are leaving right now for Times Square.
We need to **Capture** Ramón Cortez.

SARA

Of course! Mr. Martinez,
Do you want me to send an alert to all units?

EDGARDO

Do what now Vega?
Do you want all NYCPD to know that we are chasing a dead man? Do you want me to look like an idiot in front of my bosses and the media?

SARA

No boss, how do you think?
Tell me how I can help you?

EDGARDO

For now, you and I are going to Times Square
We will go to the place where Mariana had Ramón.
Javier and Zarante stay here waiting for more information.

ZARANTE

Yes boss, I'll keep you posted.

They both go out and Javier stays with Zarante in the police office.

Scene 14 - Exterior New York City - Day

Ramón arrives at a park, puts on a hoodie to cover his face. He can't believe everything that has happened, he doesn't know what to do. At that moment he receives a message from Facebook.

(Anonymous Member: Ramón Cortez, we are the Anonymous movement, the world's largest hackers, we want to help you, find us at this address: 228 N 12th St, Brooklyn, NY 11211)

Ramón is surprised, he knows that he could be a trap, but he has no other option.
When Ramón arrives at the site, he answers the message by Facebook. (I'm here now!)

LA JEFA

We're here! down the hall!

A man appears wearing an Anonymous mask, he approaches Ramón. Ramón is scared and wants to turn around and run out of that place. But at that moment a woman grabs him from behind and puts a knife to his throat, the woman is also wearing an anonymous mask.

RAMÓN

Who are you? Do not kill me! please! Do not kill me!!

LA JEFA

¡Fool! if I wanted to kill you
I would have done it by now, believe me!

Ramón punches the woman in the stomach and walks away.
Ramón tries to run away but he is stopped by the other man and they both start fighting.
Ramón knocks the man to the ground and removes his mask.

RAMÓN

Who the fuck are you?

The woman stands up and removes her mask as well, it is revealed that they are La Jefa and Franco.

LA JEFA

Oh! I finally have the pleasure to meet
the famous Ramón Cortez!

Franco is still lying on the floor, he gets up little by little.

FRANCO

You don't know who we are, but we do know everything you've done and who helped you fake your death.

Ramon walks away. La Jefa approaches Ramón.

LA JEFA

Calm down Ramón,
we know where the people you are looking for are.

FRANCO

Not only that Ramón, we want to offer you a deal.

RAMÓN

¿A deal? What deal is that?

LA JEFA

Oh Ramón, let's stop this nonsense, we know that you still have 5 million dollars in your possession, we want that money in exchange for your family.

RAMÓN

So you work for "El Jefe"

LA JEFA

Haha me? mmm mmm, I don't work for anyone! I'm doing this to show my husband who is the boss in this organization!

FRANCO

She... is the one who will give the orders from now on!...

LA JEFA

That's right, my dear Ramón,
and this is what we want to do!......

Scene 15 - Interior - Basement - Day

In the basement where Walter is, they are now with him; Carolina, Lorraine, Amelia and Emanuel, all tied up.

EMANUEL

Let go of me Wretches! Don't hurt my wife!

CHRISTOPHER

Shut up! Old asshole! here you do not give orders!

At that moment Christopher punches Emanuel.

EMANUEL

Respect me! Damn! Why do you have us here?

Trap appears and pulls the gun out of her.

TRAP

You are the key piece that is going to give us a lot of money!

LORRAINE

Money? What is happening to you? Are you stupid or what?
I already helped you with the bank robbery, what more
money do you want? I no longer have anything!
My share is with the police!

TRAP

El Jefe is coming here! You have to cover everyone's faces!

Trap and Christopher use the bags and cover their faces to all.

El Jefe walks in and lights a cigarette, and starts smoking. He starts walking slowly around all of them. He stops and looks at them one by one. Some of them are terrified, they don't know why they are there. El Jefe crouches down, bending his knee, and speaks directly to Amelia.

EL JEFE

You must be Mrs. Cortez? right?
Ramón's sister?

From the fear that terrifies her, Emilia cannot speak. But El Jefe takes the bag from Amelia's head and she says...

AMELIA

Yes... I'm Ramón's sister...
Why do they have us here? Who are you?

EL JEFE

Tell me, Mrs. Amelia, have you seen your brother somewhere recently?

AMELIA

My brother? My brother is dead!
What's wrong with you?

Says Amelia crying! The Chief smiles and continues to smoke her cigar.

EL JEFE

Oh, I see! Apparently she has not received the news!

El Jefe gets up and goes to Walter, Walter is sedated and sleeping. He kicks him to wake him up. He removes the bag from his head and tells him...

EL JEFE

¡Wake up! Police! You have company!

Walter wakes up and says:

WALTER

What? It is not my family right?
you promised you would leave them out of this!

EL JEFE

Don't worry! Walter! Why don't you tell our guests what really happened with Ramón Cortez! huh? His family is here with us!

Walter understood that if he had already told them everything, there was no sense to keep hiding the truth!

WALTER

Ramón is alive! I helped him fake his death and escape!

Walter said in a worn and embarrassed voice. At that moment Emanuel panicked and lost his patience and yelled at El Jefe.

EMANUEL

Ramón? Where is he? What did you do with him?
Leave us alone!

At that moment, Trap arrives and hits Emanuel with his knee in the chest.

TRAP

Shut up and listen you moron!

AMELIA

No... He must be lying, my brother is with God! They gave me his ashes, we picked them up at the cemetery, I almost died of pain! I wanted to die with him! It's too much pain! Why are you torturing us like this? Leave us alone! in peace! I want peace please!

After these painful words from Amelia, El Jefe did not show the slightest feeling of empathy towards her, what's more, he didn't even pay attention to what she said, he just limited himself to keep walking around them. He got in the middle of Lorena and Carolina, he knelt down and took the bag from Lorena's head and said...

EL JEFE

Your hubby is still alive and has 5 million dollars, he came out more alive than you! That asshole!

LORRAINE

Ramón? Ramón was mentally ill! He suffered from hallucinations! I don't believe you at all! I don't know what you're looking for with all this!

CAROLINA

Look stupid! I don't know who the hell you are! But what I do know is that you and all these criminals are going to go to jail and they are going to give you many years in jail!

Carolina yelled as she gathered her courage and faced El Jefe. He takes the bag off his head and tells her...

EL JEFE

Oh! How pretty you are, you must be Carolina. I'm so sorry you had to be a part of all this, it was never our plan to **capture** you, unfortunately you were on the wrong spot, at the wrong time.

CAROLINA

So! Let me go! Unfortunate!

The Chief stands up and speaks loudly.

EL JEFE

Of course I won't let you go! I won't let any of you go! I know you won't give me the money I want, but you are the bait that will make Ramón Cortez come out of his hiding place and give us the 5 million dollars that belong to us.

Then he kneels again where Carolina.

EL JEFE

Do you know something Carolina? Even if you were an accident I am very happy that you are here.

As he tells her that, he starts touching her legs. Then he stands up and tells his accomplices.

EL JEFE

I want you to untie her and take her to my room, We're going to have fun.

Trap and Christopher listen to him, El Jefe gets out of there, while they put a tape in her mouth and lift her from where she is tied up. Lorena starts screaming trying to defend her sister from them, but she is still weak, and she finds herself tied up, she feels powerless and heartbroken. Carolina starts to move and wants to scream, but the other two hold her tight.

LORRAINE

Damn! Wretches! leave my sister alone! don't touch her please! don't mess with her!

Amelia starts to panic, she starts to cry, while at the same time she starts to pray out loud.

Scene 16 - Interior Basement - Night

Hours have passed since Carolina was taken away and they haven't heard from her. The criminals returned and took the bags from everyone. We see Amelia who continues to pray out loud.
She closes her eyes and panic seizes her. From this situation, Amelia develops an episode of schizophrenia and has a hallucination. When Amelia opens her eyes again, she clearly sees Ramón lying dead on the floor in front of her. Ramón is all bloody and his face is pale. There is blood on the floor and Amelia screams in horror.

AMELIA

Ramon! my brother, you are not dead!, no, my brother you are not dead! Wake up! Come on, wake up! Wake up.

Scene 17 - Interior - The Boss House - Day

It is sunrise, and everyone is woken up by Amelia's screams.

EMILIA (2 PERSONALITY)

Amelia....Amelia....Amelia....wake up now!
they killed your husband

AMELIA

huh? What? What happened? No! No! Nooo! Emanuel! Emanuel! Nooo! He is dead! They killed him! first my brother and now my husband? Who killed my husband?

EMILIA (2 PERSONALITY)

Well who else? Amelia, who was the only one with a knife here? Well he! Look! He was the one who killed him!

Emilia points to Christopher.

AMELIA

It was you! unfortunate! you killed my Emmanuel!

CHRISTOPHER

What? No! Mrs. Amelia, I can swear that it wasn't me! I was watching all night and I didn't notice anything.

AMELIA

Well someone did! And when I find out who it was
I kill it myself!

CHRISTOPHER

This is very strange ma'am, I'm going up
to check the security cameras!

Christopher goes up and talks to Trap about what happened.

CHRISTOPHER

Hey! Trap! Somebody killed that old asshole.

TRAP

What? Who did they kill? Ramon's brother in law?
How did someone kill him? it was not you?

CHRISTOPHER

No it was not me! Why would I kill him? Those were not
the orders they gave me! He woke up dead today with knife
wounds.

TRAP

Christopher, don't be an asshole, down there the only one who had a knife was you! I already said that you killed him and that's it! Nobody cares!

CHRISTOPHER

Trap! That I have not killed him! It really wasn't me! I'm going to check the security cameras, see what happened!

Christopher tries to go inside to see the security cameras, but realizes that they are not working, and that there is no way to see what happened during the night.

CHRISTOPHER

Trap! Something is wrong with the security cameras! they are not working! there is no way to see what happened during the night!

Trap approaches to see.

TRAP

What? This is very strange!
I'm going to call Franco to see what's going on!

El Jefe hears noises and decides to go down to see what is happening.

EL JEFE

Gentlemen, what's going on?

CHRISTOPHER

Jefe, someone killed Ramon's brother in law!
Do you know anything about it?

EL JEFE

Me? Why would I have to know something? What do you think, that I killed him? Yesterday I spent the whole night with Carolina, I didn't leave the room at all.

TRAP

Boss, the other thing is that we are checking the security cameras and apparently they are not working, we do not know what is happening, I am trying to communicate with Franco.

EL JEFE

Well that is strange, keep me posted on that, also before my wife arrives let me know, I don't want her to be jealous...

CHRISTOPHER

Of course, Chief, I'll let you know! don't worry!

EL JEFE

Christopher, come down, take out the man's body, remove any evidence, we don't care who killed him, but we don't want clues that compromise us in anything.

TRAP

Jefe, don't worry, I don't know who is responsible for this, but I'll take care of this situation, don't worry!

The scene changes and we see the mysterious character watching everything that happens in the house through the security cameras.

Scene 18 - Interior - Basement - Day

Lorena despairs, she has no news from Carolina and she believes that they could have done something bad to her, so she begins to scream and ask for help. Trap goes down and starts talking to her.

TRAP

What's happening here? What are those screams?

LORRAINE

It's me! listen to me, you know that El Jefe, he is a selfish person, he only thinks of himself, when he wants to get rid of you, he will kill you, like he did with Amelia's husband!

TRAP

Linda, we are aware of that and believe me I am not going to let any of that happen to any of us.

LORRAINE

Help me with Carolina, please, don't let him hurt her, I'm capable of doing anything, anything, for her to be okay.

TRAMPA

Are you willing to do anything? Yeah? How much would you do to free Carolina from this?

LORRAINE

Whatever I have to do for my sister's sake, I'll do it!

Trappa bends over and begins to caress Lorena.

TRAP

You know? If you're nice to me, I can help you escape. You are a beautiful woman, and things can be better for you

LORRAINE

Release me from here, and I'll let you do whatever you want to me, I'll be yours if you want to, just help us escape!

TRAP

Ok, I'll let you go and I'll get you out of here,
But first I want to spend some time with you.

LORRAINE

It's okay, but take me to where they have Carolina, don't let them hurt her.

Christopher comes down and tells Amelia:

CHRISTOPHER

Something happened to the security cameras, they're not working! I have to take the body and clean everything!

AMELIA

Ah, certainly! Now it turns out that the only way to see who killed my husband doesn't work! How convenient! huh?

CHRISTOPHER

Ma'am, believe me we don't understand how it's not working either!

AMELIA

And now you're going to take it to clean everything up and cover your tracks and all the evidence, right?

CHRISTOPHER

Think what you want! Crazy old woman! I still have to take the dead man and get him out of here!

At that moment, Trap frees Lorena, but still keeps her hands tied, grabs her by her arm and takes her out of the basement, taking her up to the 1st floor of the house.
Trap takes Lorena to a room.

TRAP

Well! We are both alone!

yes! lovely! you will see what's good!

Trap begins to kiss and caress her. He starts to take off his clothes.

LORRAINE

You know? If you let go of my hands, I will be able to touch all that chest, and give you some caresses that you will not be able to forget in your life.

TRAP

I will let you go, I will trust you. I want you! But we can't make too much noise, we're not too far from the other rooms.

LORRAINE

Sure baby! What's your name?

TRAP

The less you know about us the better! but I also want you not to forget about me and all the fun we are going to have, people call me El Trampa, sweetheart.

At that moment Lorena is completely free, she lifts her blouse and turns her back to Trampa, he begins to kiss her back.

TRAP

Turn around sweetheart, let's see those breasts!

Lorena stealthily takes a bottle of beer and quickly turns around and smashes it over Trappa's head.

LORRAINE

Forgive me, Trap, I like you, but I do this for my family. It's not the moment.

Trap falls unconscious to the floor and Lorena takes the opportunity to leave the room and look for Carolina.

Scene 19 - Interior - El Jefe's House - Day

La Jefa arrives with Ramón (who is bound and gagged, unable to speak) in his possession he has a bag full of money, which Ramón gave her to free his family. Franco goes after Ramón, guiding him, since he has his head covered with a bag so that he does not know the location of the house.
La Jefa sees that something is wrong in the house, she doesn't see her husband, and there is no one guarding the entrances of it.

LA JEFA

Something is wrong here Franco, prepare for the worst, this is going to get ugly, I can feel it.

FRANCO

Don't worry boss, go up and see what's happening, I'll stay here with Ramón, checking the servers and security cameras.

Ramón makes noises with his mouth.

FRANCO

I'm going to free you, calm down!

Franco takes away the moorings he has. La Jefa goes up to the second floor, and Franco takes the bag off Ramón's head and starts checking the security cameras.

FRANCO

How odd! indeed someone has hacked us! Someone has taken over the security cameras and wanted to steal information from us!

RAMÓN

Is there a way to recover the recordings from the cameras?

FRANCO

Of course! Nothing is impossible for me! In a matter of seconds I will be able to see what happened!

They both begin to see the recordings of the security cameras. They watch as Trap takes Lorena out of the basement.

RAMÓN

That! It's my wife Lorraine! Do you know where they went? Where will they be now?

FRANCO

They are likely in the Trap Room.
It is at the bottom left.

Ramón heads in that direction and after a moment he finds himself face to face with Lorraine. They both look into each other's eyes, Lorraine is paralyzed without moving, she can't believe that she has her husband in front of her who until a few days ago she thought he was dead.

LORRAINE

Ramon! Is it you? Are you alive?

RAMÓN

Lorraine! my love! Are you OK?

Ramón approaches and hugs Lorena. Then he looks into her eyes and wants to kiss her but she rejects him and slaps him and pushes him back with her arms.

LORRAINE

Good? How do you want me to be good, Ramón Cortez?
Not even dead, you can do things right!

RAMÓN

Love! I came back to rescue them all!

LORRAINE

Well look! I have been on the verge of death! after waking up from a coma, they put me in jail! and then they kidnap me and my sister for money that you still had.

RAMÓN

Lore, forgive me, I didn't want things to happen like this!

LORRAINE

And now I don't know what the hell they are doing to Caro! How do you want me to be okay?

RAMÓN

Carolina? What happened to her? Where is she?

LORRAINE

The wretch, damn, that El Jefe, like he wants to rape her! but that son of a ***** is going to pay me for all of them!

RAMÓN

Look! his wife, La Jefa, has a plan! Do not do anything that endangers your life, or Carolina's, where is my sister?

LORRAINE

She is in the basement, along with Walter. But something happened...I don't want to tell you, you better go and see it for yourself.

RAMÓN

What? What happened? I'm going right now, but let's do this, take this knife, and wait for me here, while I go get a weapon, and we go down to the basement to free them.

LORRAINE

Come on, I'll wait for you here.

Scene 20 - Interior House - The Boss - Day

At that moment, the mysterious character, who we had been seeing previously, appears outside El Jefe's house, this time we see his face and we see an eagle tattoo on his hand, he has the key that opens the front door, enters and goes to the room where Trap is.

EAGLE

Trap! Trap! wake up! We have to end the plans we have!

TRAP

huh? What happened? Eagle?
Is it you? What happened to me?

EAGLE

It happened to you, that Lorena hit you on the head with a bottle! I saw it all through the cameras.

TRAP

Damn! She cheated me! But this does not stay like that!
That bastard is going to pay me!

EAGLE

Then you take care of it! Now we need the databases of the banks to be able to rob them without them realizing it!

TRAP

Yeah! of course! That's how it is! Franco has that information, let's go and talk to him.

They both arrive where Franco is.

FRANCO

Trap! I know what happened! Apparently someone hacked us! seized the security cameras! and tried to steal important information from us.

At that moment, Trap approaches Franco from behind, pulls out a gun and points it at Franco's head.

TRAP

Listen to me! You have two options, either accept what we are going to propose, or I'll kill you right now! That person who hacked us is right here! I present to you, he is my friend The Eagle! The boss of bosses!

EAGLE

From now on, I'm the one who gives the orders in this organization, you just do what I tell you to do, or you die right here! you understand?

Franco raises his hands and says:

FRANCO

Alright! Alright! no problem! I accept, you just tell me what you want me to do! and I'll do it right away!

EAGLE

I need the database with all the passwords and access codes, from the largest banks in the world, we are going to rob them penny by penny without them noticing.

TRAP

That's right, Ramón's 5 million are nothing compared to the billions of dollars that we are going to have with that database!

FRANCO

That database, it's encrypted so strongly it's going to take me hours to crack it.

EAGLE

Well, you don't get out of here alive and we won't leave until we have it in our possession, so get to work now!

FRANCO

Alright! I will try to do it as fast as possible!

Scene 21 - Interior - Basement - Day

Ramón takes out the cell phone that Mariana gave him, tries to call her and she doesn't answer.

RAMÓN

What 's happening? Mariana answer!

Seeing that she doesn't answer, he starts looking through the cell phone contacts and finds Javier's number and calls him.

JAVIER

Hello? Mariana? Who's there?

RAMÓN

I'm Ramon Cortez, Mariana gave me this phone to communicate with her. Where is she?

JAVIER

Ramón Cortez? Where are you?
all the police are looking for you!

RAMÓN

I am at the house of the Head of the criminal hacker organization. I am collaborating with justice as we had agreed, I will send you my location. We need them to come for us.

JAVIER
The police have you as a suspect in Mariana's death.

RAMÓN
What? What are you talking about? She left the hotel where we were, because she got a call from you.

JAVIER
Don't you know what happened to Mariana?

RAMÓN
What? What happened to her?

JAVIER
Mariana was murdered in Times Square,
right after she left the Hotel!

RAMÓN
What? Who did that?

JAVIER
Everything is under investigation, send me your address
And I'll notify director Martinez.

After this call, Ramón finds the entrance to the basement, opens the door, but instead of going down, he throws an object down the stairs, as a way of seeing who is there. (the noise of the object falling down the stairs is heard)

CHRISTOPHER

What's that? Who's there?

AMELIA

Help! Help us! We are CAPTURED!

CHRISTOPHER

Shut up, you crazy old woman!
Do you think they are going to come and rescue you?

AMELIA

Help! They killed my husband! don't let us die here!

CHRISTOPHER

I'm going to cover that snout, so that it stops making noise!

Amelia continues making noises with her mouth, Walter is next to her but he is in an unconscious state, they gave him something to make him fall asleep and lose consciousness.
Christopher goes up the stairs, opens the door, at that moment, Ramón hits him in the face, and Christopher falls to the floor, Ramón gets on top of him, and he goes crazy and begins to hit Christopher brutally and without stall.
Christopher loses consciousness and Ramón goes down to the basement to free his sister and Walter.

RAMÓN

Sister! Are you OK?

AMELIA

My God! you heard my prayers! Thanks my Lord!

RAMÓN

What happened to Emmanuel?

AMELIA

Thank God you're alive!
Emanuel was killed by these bastards!

RAMÓN

What? Who killed him? Tell me everything you know!

AMELIA

Ramon! the only thing I know! and I remember is that I woke up and found him with knife wounds! Someone killed him while we were sleeping, they went to check the security cameras, but they weren't working!

RAMÓN

Look, this is the plan, I already told the police where we are, reinforcements are coming. We have a plan to take down El Jefe. But I promise you that I will get you out of here alive.

Ramón takes out and turns on a small cell phone that he had hidden, and sends a message with the location to Javier.

Message: Javier, I found El Jefe's house, where the prisoners are, send reinforcements. It's time to face the consequences of the decisions I've made.

Scene 22 - Interior - House The Boss - Day

La Jefa goes up to the second floor of the house, and hears screams coming from a room, she tries to open the door but it is locked, she takes her keys and opens the door.

LA JEFA

Damn, leave her alone!

EL JEFE

Maria! do not get into this! It's your fault that I'm doing what I'm doing!

LA JEFA

What? What are you saying? Now it turns out that I am the one to blame for all the women you have raped, because of that crazy desire to have a child?

EL JEFE

Yeah! That's how it is! If you had given me the son I've always wanted, I wouldn't have to do all that you say I've done.

LA JEFA

¡Fool! And it doesn't occur to you that YOU are to blame for YOU not being able to have children? huh? That the sterile one is YOU wretch!

EL JEFE

Me? I'm a stallion, what's wrong with you? Of course it can't be me!

LA JEFA

Stallion... What's wrong with me? Pedro Jose? What happens to me is, I'm sick of you, and everything you've done, because everything you've done, you've done wrong!

EL JEFE

Don't say my name in front of her, besides, What are you talking about?

LA JEFA

What I mean is, up to here, I'm with you, from now on I am the one who will take care of everything.

La Jefa pulls out a gun and points it at El Jefe. At that moment, Lorraine arrives in the room, and she takes La Jefa by surprise from behind. The gun falls to the floor and the two begin to fight to see who gets the gun. Meanwhile, El Jefe pulls out a knife and has Carolina held with the knife to her throat.

Lorraine manages to take the gun, stands up and points it at them.

LORRAINE

I don't know what the hell is going on between you two, but I need Carolina to be handed over to me right now!

LA JEFA

You must be Lorena, Ramón's wife, right?

LORRAINE

And who the hell are you?

LA JEFA

I, my dear, am the new head of this organization, and the only way to get out of here with your sister is if you kill him, now!

EL JEFE

Lorraine, listen to me! I am and will continue to be the head of this organization! If you want Carolina alive, drop that weapon, now!

LORRAINE

You are not going to tell me what I have to do! okay? I want Carolina with me now! Or I'll shoot her and then you!

At that moment Carolina hits El Jefe in the eyes, and Carolina ducks, she takes the opportunity to run away, and Lorraine fires the first shot at El Jefe.

El Jefe falls to the ground from a shot to the chest. Then Lorraine points to La Jefa and says:

LORRAINE

Now you're going to let us out of here,
If not, I'll give you another bullet too!

LA JEFA

¡Go ahead and try! go! try to run away! Without my help you won't be able to go very far, remember that you are an accomplice to the bank robbery, you have a warrant for your arrest, and you have just killed a man.

CAROLINA

She's right, sister, what are you going to do now?

LORRAINE

The important thing is that you are well!
Don't worry about me.

LA JEFA

You've worked for us before, and you did me a favor by killing him. Do you want to go to jail for the rest of your life?

LORRAINE

Of course not! Ma'am, but I, I can say that you forced me to do all this, I will be a victim of your criminal organization, which I am going to help bring to justice.

LA JEFA

Oh yeah? and how do you plan to do that? huh?

At that moment Carolina bends over, and she takes the knife that her boss had and stabs her boss in her leg, which makes her fall to the floor, and hit a huge scream.

At that moment they both take the opportunity to run out of there.

LORRAINE

Carolina, you're free now, and you have to run away from here, you can't be next to me, it's dangerous!

CAROLINA

Sister, I don't want to leave you alone!
Come with me! Let's get out of here now!

LORRAINE

No Carolina, I still have things to do here, look at this, here is the address of a place where you can go, they will protect you and you will be safe, when I can I will communicate with you, through them, okay?

CAROLINA

Alright! I will go! but I want you to promise me that you will be fine, and that you will communicate with me, as soon as possible, okay?

LORRAINE

yeah, sis, count on it!

They hug and Carolina runs away from the site. Lorraine stays watching as she manages to escape from there.

Scene 23 - Interior - El Jefe's House - Day

While Franco is working on decrypting the database, he receives a notification that the police are nearby.

FRANCO

Gentlemen, I just received a notification, the police are heading towards this place! in less than 15 minutes they will be here.

EAGLE

Are you done with decoding the database?

FRANCO

Of course not! I told you that I need hours! what do you think? If it were that easy, everyone would have that in their power!

TRAP

What do we do, Eagle? Shall we go without it? or what?

EAGLE

Of course we're leaving, but Franco is coming with us, and with all his equipment! we are going to finish that decoding sooner or later, but we are going to have it!
we will have it!

FRANCO

Yeah! It's possible, I can take the laptops and hard drives and continue with this later, we don't have much time to get out of here!

At that moment Lorraine arrives and meets Trap.

LORRAINE

Trap! I need your help! Help me! please!

TRAP

Oh yeah? And why would I have to help you? If everything was clear to me, after the blow you gave me, ahh?

LORRAINE

Excuse me, I don't know why I reacted like this! I just killed El Jefe! I shot that bastard!

TRAP

Oh! And what do you want me to give you an award for that? huh?

LORRAINE

No! but I don't want to spend years in jail! I wouldn't stand it! You and I have something pending, remember! This time I am going to fulfill you! But help me run away with you!

EAGLE

Trap! We have to go now! They are waiting for us!

Trap approaches the Eagle and says:

TRAP

Eagle! Lorraine is coming with us!
She is going to help us with this!

EAGLE

If you want to bring that bitch! bring it to you!
but we have to go now!

Trap goes back to talk to Lorena and says:

TRAP

Alright! You come with us! But don't think it's going to be that easy, we have plans and you're going to help us with that! Do you agree?

LORRAINE

Yeah! I agree! You won't regret this, believe me.

TRAP

I hope so! You better be nice to me!
or you won't have much luck next time.

At that moment the 4 leave the house as fast as they can. Police siren sounds are heard, the 4 run until they find a helicopter that is waiting for them.

TRAP

Get on everyone, I'll make sure these damn policemen don't hurt us.

Trap starts shooting at the cops.

EAGLE

Trap! It's now or never! we're leaving now!
you get on or stay!

TRAP

Ready! we can go now!
These bastards are not going to bother us anymore!

The helicopter takes off and is seen as they fly away in the air.

Scene 24 - El Jefe's House - Day

At this moment, Ramón is coming out of the basement with his sister and Walter. Christopher is found unconscious, lying on the floor. Everyone gathers in the room.

At that moment, the police enter the house. The police come in and talk to everyone in the room.

ZARANTE
Boss, everyone is here!

EDGARD
Gentlemen, what happened here? How are you?

AMELIA
Officer, they kidnapped us, they killed my husband!
and some ran away! My brother rescued me!

SARAH
Walter, are you okay? We were worried about you.

WALTER
I'm fine, they tortured me, but Ramón came to free us.

ZARANTE
Ramon, how are you? Alright?

RAMÓN

Thank God we are fine, thanks to you for coming to look for us.

SARA

Ramón, remember that you must turn yourself in to the police, it is better to clarify everything, if you want to get out of this well.

RAMÓN

I know officer, we hope that now all this ends as it should.

JAVIER

Mr. Cortez, come over for a moment, please.

RAMÓN

Yes tell me, what happened?

JAVIER

Outside is your ex-wife Angelica, she is helping us. We know about your illness and we want to help you.

RAMÓN

Thanks, can I talk to her?

JAVIER

Of course! follow me.

Javier takes him to one of the cars that is outside the house, opens the back door and Angelica gets out of the car.

ANGELICA

Ramón, first of all I want you to know that I understand you, I forgive you, and I apologize.

RAMÓN

Angelica, no, excuse me! You know better than anyone how someone with my disease reacts, I need your help to move forward.

ANGELICA

Ramón, now you are going to start a difficult and harsh process with the courts of this country, that is why I am going to give you this, it is your good luck bracelet, remember?

RAMÓN

Wow, of course I do, the last time I had it, well... I don't remember very well.

ANGELICA

The important thing is that when you feel like you can't take it anymore, hold on to this and remember all the good things you've done for yourself, your family and everyone around you.

RAMÓN

Thank you, you can't imagine how much I'm going to value this moment, I'll remember it for the rest of my life, thank you.

RAMÓN

Angelica, will I ever be cured of schizophrenia?

ANGELICA

Ramón, if you believe it is possible in your mind, it will be so! Ask God! Pray a lot, for him everything is possible.

At that moment, officer Sara comes out and tells Ramón that she should come into the house because they found something important.

SARA

Mr. Cortez, come closer, please,
Detective Martinez found something important and he needs you to see it.

RAMÓN

Come, come with me, let's go inside for a moment.

Ramón enters the house with Dr. Angelica. When his sister enters, Amelia is handcuffed and crying.

EDGARDO

Mr. Cortez, we were finally able to access the security cameras and we've found something you need to see.

In the video it is clearly seen when Amelia, in a state of hallucination, gets up from her, takes the knife from Christopher, approaches her where her husband is and begins to stab him.

Ramón doesn't know what to do... nor say... his sister is a murderer.
The camera changes and now Ramón is next to Amelia.

RAMÓN

Amelia? was it you? Did you kill your own husband? why? Why did you do it?

AMELIA

Little brother! ¡No! It was Emily! Yes, it was her!

EMILIA (2 PERSONALITY)

Oh! Amelia! Now they are going to think that you are crazy, crazy, crazy!

AMELIA

You know who she is! right? She told me that she killed Emanuel! you see her too right?

EMILIA (2 PERSONALITY)

Poor Amelia, look at you, ending up like this! Obviously they don't see me, and nobody believes you...ha ha ha...

Amelia is in a state of shock.

EDGARDO

Mr. Cortez, calm down, obviously her sister is suffering from some kind of hallucination, very surely it is the reason why you also have the same disease.

SARA

Ramón, calm down, calm down, your sister must be transferred right now, we will contact you to give you more information.

The policemen take Amelia into custody, while Ramón is taken away for questioning.

Scene 25 - Various Locations - (Walter's voiceover)

Many things happened after the events of El Jefe's house, La Jefa was **captured** along with Christopher, they face a sentence of 20 years in prison.

El Jefe died and was buried alone, with no one visiting him.

Carolina became pregnant as a result of the rape of which she was the victim. Carolina did not want that baby and she gave it up for adoption.

Amelia was sentenced for the death of her husband and was admitted to a psychiatric clinic.

Ramón was acquitted of everything, but he understood that he needed to heal and be emotionally well, so he decided to try to reconcile and resume his relationship with his ex-wife, now they both live together, support and help each other.

Scene 26 - Post Credits 1 - Exterior - Beach/Pool

Lorena is lying on a chair sunbathing on a beach/pool when Trap arrives.

LORRAINE

This is the life that I deserve! right my love?

TRAP

Of course! This is the life we deserve!

LORRAINE

Look! I'm hungry! I'm craving mmm
I don't know something like an exotic fruit!
I don't know why I have these cravings!

TRAP

What exotic fruit do you want now?
Hey! It will not be that you... haha you know!

LORRAINE

What? Trap? you think that I am..? nooo.

TRAP

Well, let's get out of doubt!

I'll bring you a pregnancy test right now!

LORRAINE

Oh my gosh good! Let's get out of doubt!

Minutes later....

LORRAINE

Trap! trap! omg! Positive! I'm pregnant!

TRAP

My Love! We are going to be parents!

you make me so happy!

Scene 27 - Post Credits 2 - Interior - Jail Women -

POLICE JAIL

Mrs. Maria Cantillo, you have a visit from your lawyer.

LA JEFA

My lawyer? Which lawyer?

FRANCO

It 's me! Mrs. Maria, your trusted lawyer.

LA JEFA

Wow, wow, you finally show up....
mr... hacker... What the hell are you doing here?

FRANCO

Jefa, everything is ready, for you to come out tonight, here is your new ID, you have to change your look, there you have all the money you will need, and the indications of how we are going to do it.

LA JEFA

Ok, when I get out of here, I want
have Pedro Jose's son with me.

FRANCO

Don't worry boss, we already have the people who will receive the child for adoption.

LA JEFA

Then I want to make those imbeciles to pay for everything they did to us, Anonymous is Back!

FRANCO

Anonymous is back!

Made in the USA
Middletown, DE
03 August 2023

35893958R00070